CHICKEN
LITTLE

THE REAL AND TOTALLY TRUE TALE

SAM WEDELICH

SCHOLASTIC INC.

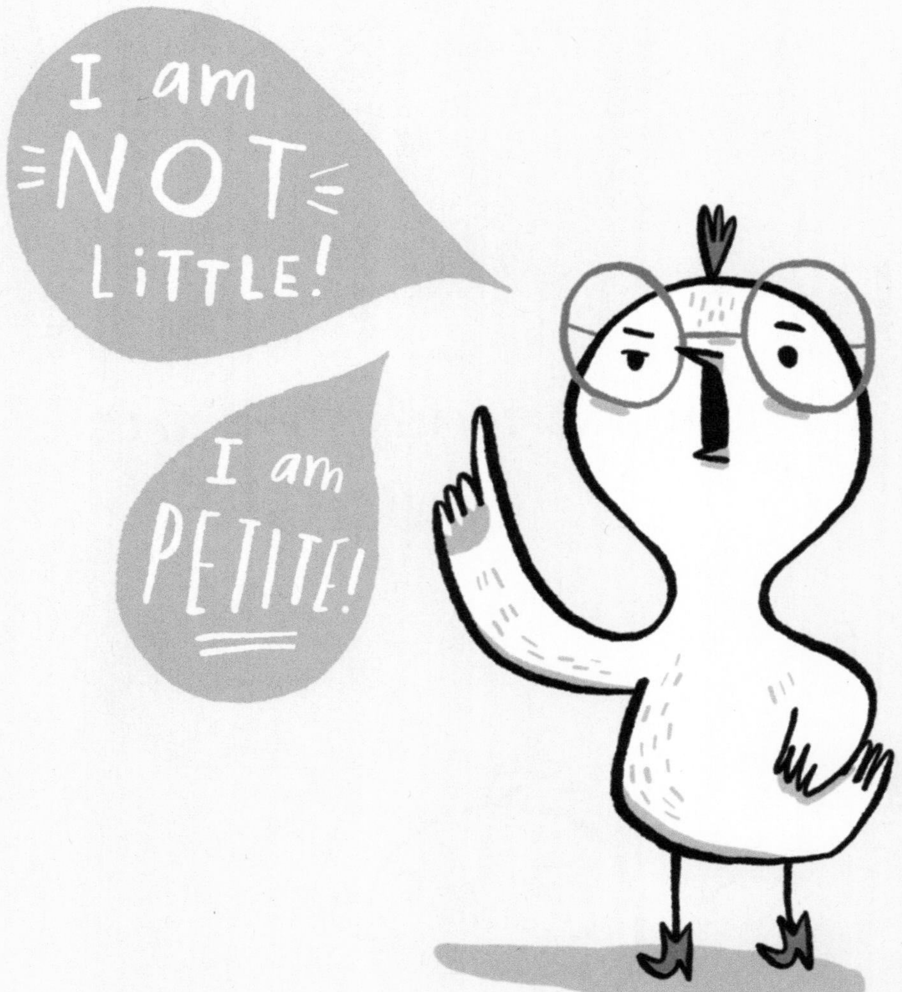
I am NOT LiTTLE!
I am PETITE!

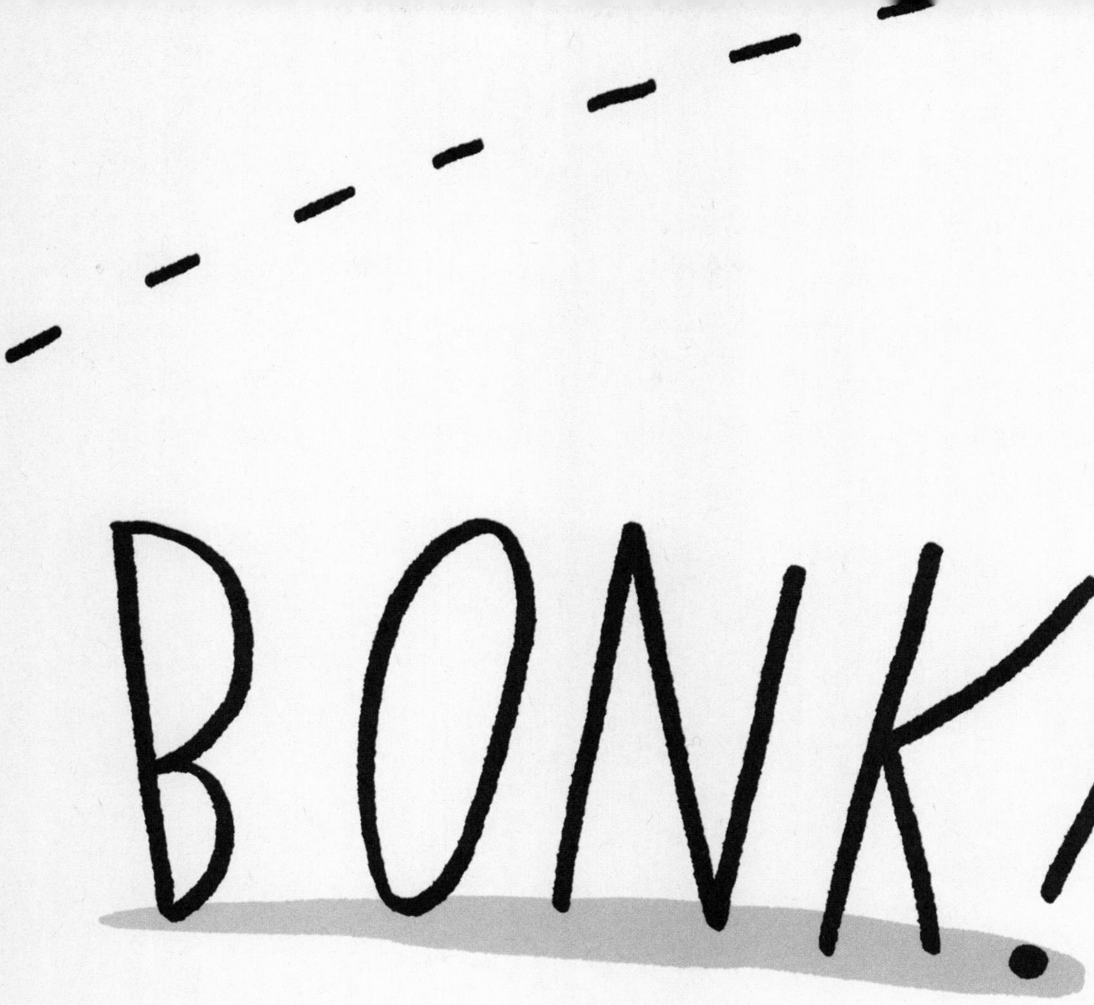
BONK!

WHAT WAS THAT?!

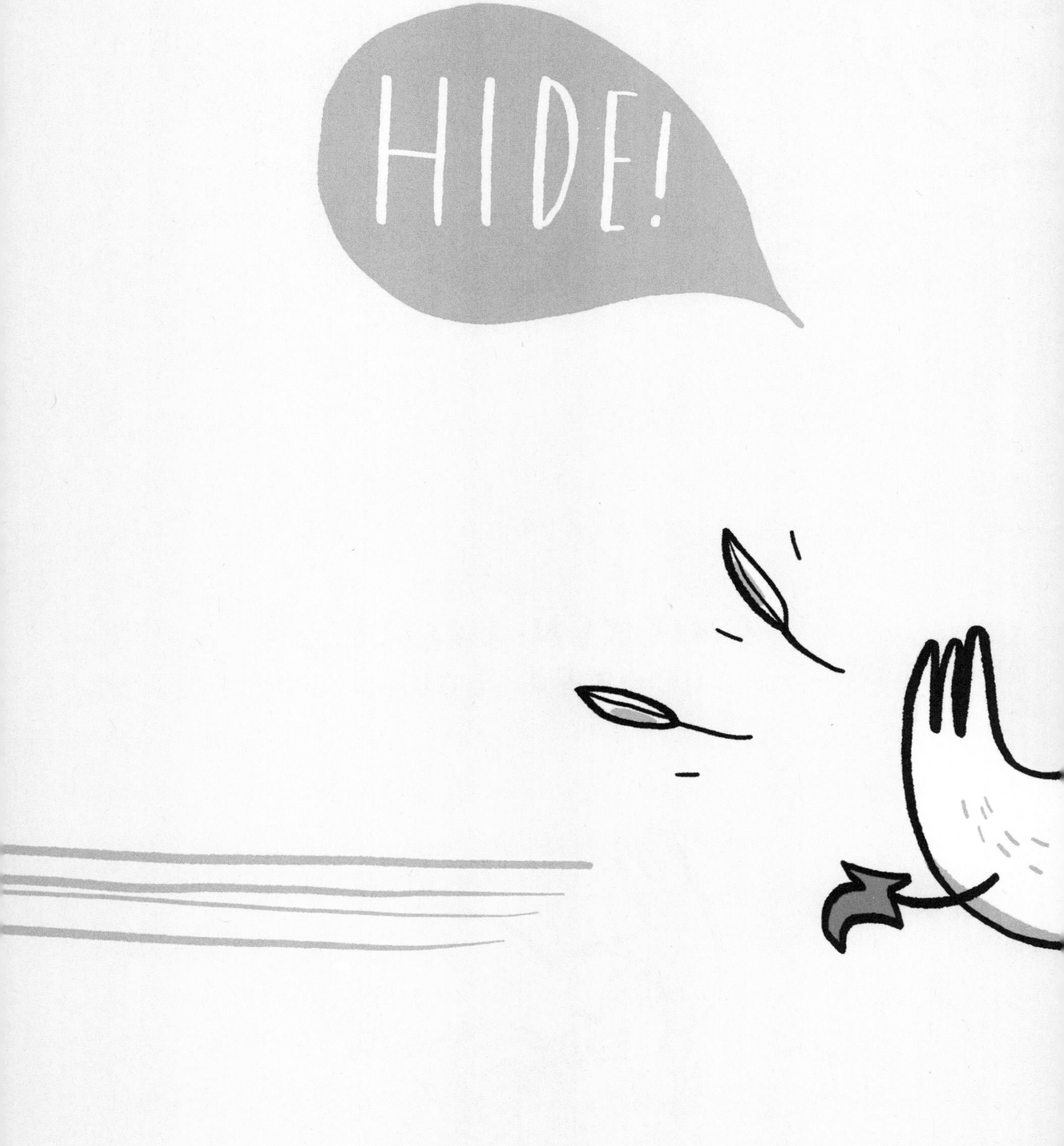
HIDE!

IS THE COAST CLEAR? NOTHING LOOKS DANGEROUS?

CHICKEN LITTLE LOOKED LOW.

CHICKEN LITTLE
LOOKED HIGH.

ME? NO!
I AM A BLANKET
OF GAS HELD by
THE PULL OF GRAVITY.
I DO NOT FALL.

JUST CHECKING IN WITH THE SKY TO MAKE SURE IT'S NOT FALLING.
WHAT?! THE SKY IS FALLING?!

THE SKY IS FALLING!

RUN! RUN!! RUN!!!

THE SKY IS
RUUUUUUUUU

CHICKEN LITTLE BROUGHT in the FACT-CHECKING SNIPES, WHO WERE WIDELY RESPECTED, BUT the HORDE of HENS WOULD'NT STOP TO LISTEN.

CHICKEN LITTLE TRIED to CORRAL THEM INTO THE COOP SO SHE COULD EXPLAIN.

BUT THE CHICKENS REFUSED to BE CAGED.

THINGS REALLY GOT OUT OF HAND WHEN CHICKEN LITTLE HEARD THE HENS CHANTING "CUT THE FENCE! CUT THE FENCE!"

"CLUCK CLUCK"
I'VE GOT ICE!
CHECK the PUPILS FOR DILATION!
"CLUCK CLUCK"

AND SHE WAS.

SEE?! TOLD YOU I WASN'T AFRAID OF ANYTHING!

For Max + Alistair + Russ

• • •

ISBN 978-1-338-71609-2 • 10 9 8 7 6 5   22 23 24 • Printed in the U.S.A.   40 • First printing, 2020
Sam Wedelich's illustrations were created digitally. • The type was hand lettered by Sam Wedelich. • The set type is Amatic Regular. Production was overseen by Catherine Weening. • Manufacturing was supervised by Shannon Rice. • The book was art directed and designed by Marijka Kostiw and edited by Tracy Mack..